Alexander's Outing

Other books by Pamela Allen

Mr McGee and the Blackberry Jam

Belinda

Mr McGee Goes to Sea

Black Dog

I Wish I Had a Pirate Suit

Fancy That!

Mr McGee

Herbert and Harry

Bertie and the Bear

Who Sank the Boat?

Mr Archimedes' Bath

Simon Said

Simon Did

Watch Me

Watch Me Now

British Library Cataloguing in Publication Data

A catalogue record for this book is available
from the British Library

ISBN 0 340 60001 2

First published 1993 by Penguin Books Australia Ltd
First published in Great Britain 1994

Published by Hodder and Stoughton Children's Books,
a division of Hodder and Stoughton Ltd,
Mill Road, Dunton Green, Sevenoaks, Kent TN13 2YA

Printed in Hong Kong through Bookbuilders Limited

Alexander's Outing

Pamela Allen

HODDER AND STOUGHTON
LONDON SYDNEY AUCKLAND

Alexander lived with his mother and his four
brothers and sisters in the most beautiful
place in the whole of Sydney, but Alexander's
mother was bored.
So one warm sunny morning they all set out
in search of adventure,

past the bottle tree,

through the iron gates

and along Art Gallery Road.

'Stay close, take care!' quacked Alexander's
mother, but Alexander did not stay close
and Alexander did not take care.
He straggled behind with his head in the air.

In College Street a man rushed out and stopped the traffic.

'Stay close, take care!' quacked Alexander's mother, but Alexander did not stay close and Alexander did not take care.

He straggled behind and he did not hear.

By the time they reached the other side
Alexander had disappeared.

Alexander's mother quacked and quacked.
'Alexander! Alexander!'
And all his brothers and sisters quacked
and quacked and flapped and flapped,
but they couldn't find Alexander anywhere.

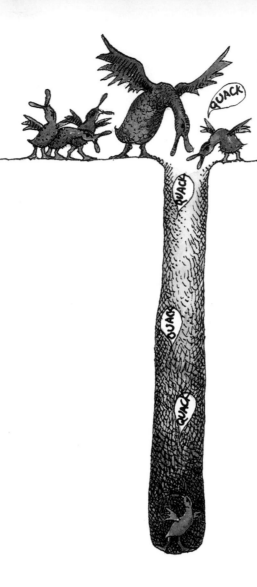

When they stopped making such a din
they heard a faint and distant 'Quack!'
from deep down in the earth.

A young man and a middle-aged lady
came over to see what was going on.

The young man tried to reach Alexander
but his long arms were not long enough.

The middle-aged lady had an umbrella.
So the young man tried again with his long
arms *and* the umbrella, but they weren't
long enough either.

A young couple picnicking in Hyde Park
heard all the commotion, packed up
their basket and came over to see what
all the fuss was about.

'How are we going to get him out?'
the middle-aged lady asked.
The young couple had no idea.
'Cheer up,' they called out, and
dropped a half-eaten cheese
sandwich down the hole.

A policeman arrived.
He knew exactly what to do.
He lowered his whistle down the hole
on the end of a long piece of string.
'Here,' he shouted. 'Grab hold of this!'

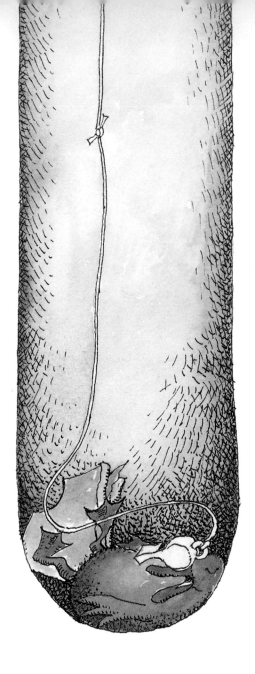

But Alexander did not grab hold.
Alexander did not hear.

A small boy and his mother joined the crowd.
A feeble 'Quack!' came from deep down in the hole.
How *were* they going to get him out?

Then before anyone could stop him,
the small boy tipped his drink down the hole.
'YAAH! Now you've gone and drowned the
poor little blighter,' shouted the young man
with the long arms.

And they all tried to peer down
the deep dark hole to see.

Everyone started talking at once.
They all wanted to rescue Alexander,
but how were they going to do it?

From their basket the young picnickers
handed out two cups, two plastic bags,
one lunch box and one thermos flask.
The small boy still held his empty drink can.

Then, ducks and all, they pranced in one
long snaky line to the Archibald fountain.

Now, dipping and tipping, dipping and tipping, skipping and dripping, quacking and flapping, dripping and skipping,

from the fountain to the hole
and back again they danced.

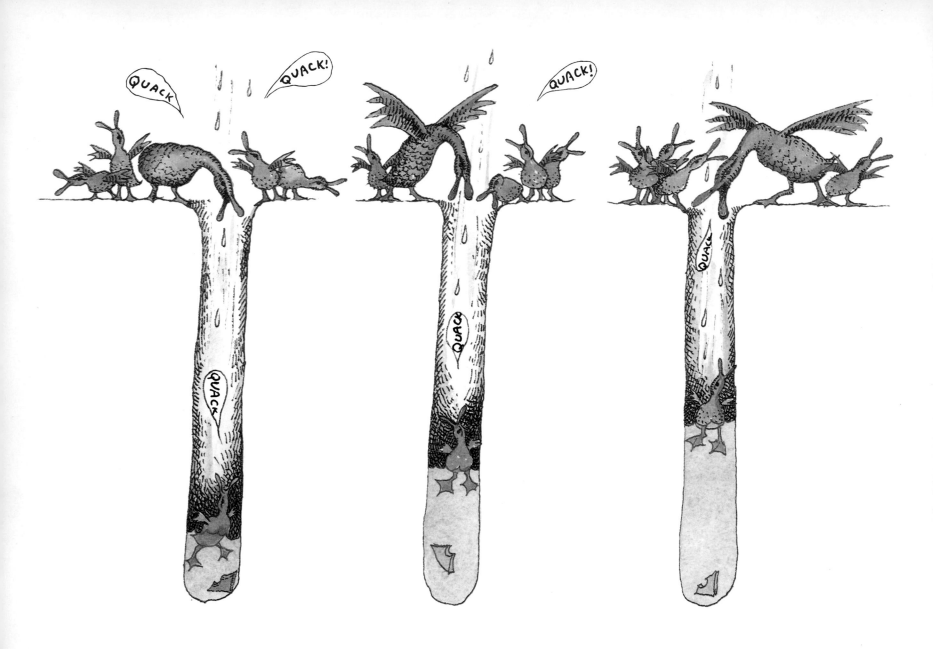

Slowly the water rose...

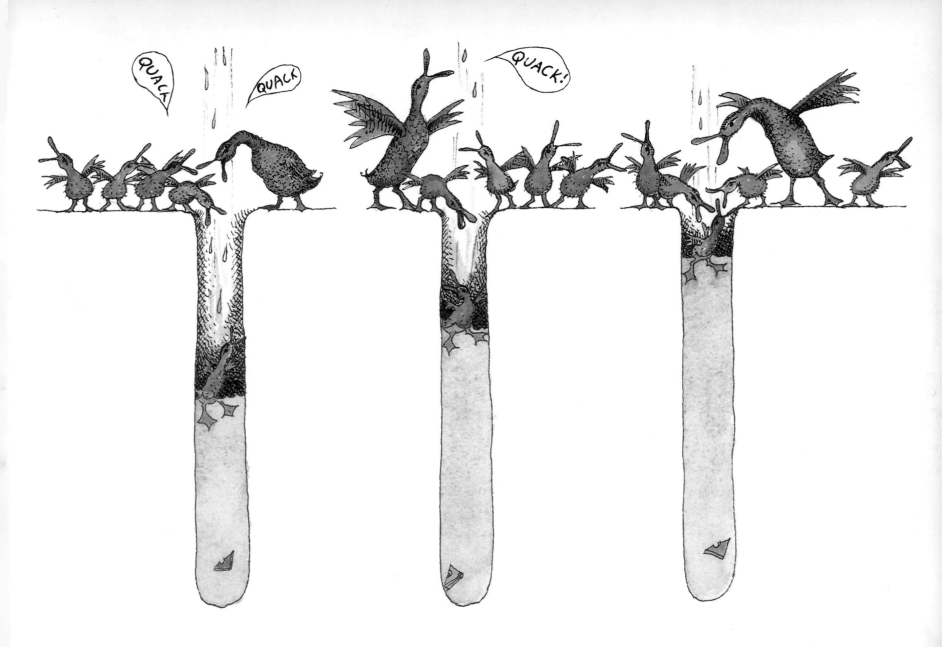

up and up and up... until...

Out popped Alexander like the cork
out of a bottle.
His mother flapped and flapped and
quacked and quacked, and all his
brothers and sisters flapped and
flapped and quacked and quacked.

Such joyful quacking!
Such happy flapping!

When the celebrations were over
they set off, still quacking and flapping,

back across College Street,

along Art Gallery Road,